THIS BOOK BELONGS TO

_____

Breakfast-Time for
THOMAS
A Thomas the Tank Engine Storybook

Based on *The Railway Series* by the Rev. W. Awdry

Illustrated by Owain Bell

Random House New York

Copyright © 1990 and 1998 by Reed International Books, Ltd. All rights reserved.
Published in the United States by Random House, Inc.
All publishing rights: Reed International Books, Ltd., London.
All television and merchandising rights licensed by Reed International Books Ltd.
to Britt Allcroft (Thomas) Ltd. Originally published in different form in 1990.
Library of Congress Catalog Card Number: 98-65583
First Random House Jellybean Books™ edition, 1998.
ISBN: 0-679-89237-0 (trade); 0-679-99237-5 (lib. bdg.)
JELLYBEAN BOOKS is a trademark of Random House, Inc.
www.randomhouse.com/kids/
Printed in the United States of America 10 9 8 7 6 5 4 3 2 1

Thomas the Tank Engine was a Really Useful Engine. He was so useful that he was given his very own Branch Line to run on.

"You could almost go without me now!" joked his driver with a laugh.

"My driver says I don't need him now," Thomas bragged to the other engines.

"You wouldn't *dare* go out without your driver," said Percy, the little green engine.

"I might," said Thomas. "Just wait and see!"

It was dark the next morning when the firelighter
came. He lit a fire in Thomas's firebox to start the fuel
burning.

Thomas woke up. Percy and the other engines were
still fast asleep.

Thomas suddenly remembered his boast.

"I'll show them!" he said. "My driver hasn't come yet. Here goes!"

He tried first one piston, then the other.

"They're moving," he whispered to himself.

Very, very quietly, he headed for the door.

Thomas thought he was being clever, but he was only moving because a careless cleaner had meddled with his controls.

When Thomas tried to stop, he couldn't. He just kept rolling along.

"The buffers will stop me," Thomas said hopefully. But his wheels left the rails and crunched on the pavement. "Oh, no!" he exclaimed, and shut his eyes.

Up ahead was the stationmaster's house. He and his family were inside, having a breakfast of ham and eggs.

Crash! The house rocked. Broken glass tinkled, and falling plaster peppered the family's plates.

And guess whose head was poking through the wall, looking in?

The stationmaster angrily walked out and shut off
Thomas's steam.

"Just look at what you've done to our breakfast!"
scolded the stationmaster's wife. "Now we shall have to
cook some more."

She banged the door on her way to the kitchen. More
plaster fell on Thomas.

Thomas felt sad. The plaster tickled his nose. He wanted to sneeze, but he didn't dare in case the house fell on him!

Nobody came for a long time. Everyone was much too busy.

At last workers propped up the house with strong poles. Then they laid rails through the garden. Puffing hard, the twin engines Donald and Douglas managed to haul Thomas back to the yard.

Thomas's smokestack was bent. Bits of fence, a bush, and a broken window frame decorated his badly twisted front. He looked quite silly!

The twin engines laughed and left him. Thomas knew he had behaved badly.

Sir Topham Hatt, the railway controller, came by to take a look. "You are a very naughty engine," he said to Thomas.

"I know, sir," Thomas said. "I'm sorry, sir."

"You must have your front mended," Sir Topham Hatt said. "Meanwhile, a diesel will do your work."

"A d-d-diesel?" Thomas spluttered in surprise.

"Yes, Thomas. Diesels *always* stay in their sheds. Diesels never run off to breakfast in stationmasters' houses," said Sir Topham Hatt.

A diesel came the next day to help out. At first he didn't want to stay in the engine shed. But he soon got used to working with the other engines.

Finally, Thomas came back, all mended and ready for work. He and the diesel became good friends. And now Thomas knows not to run off without his driver!

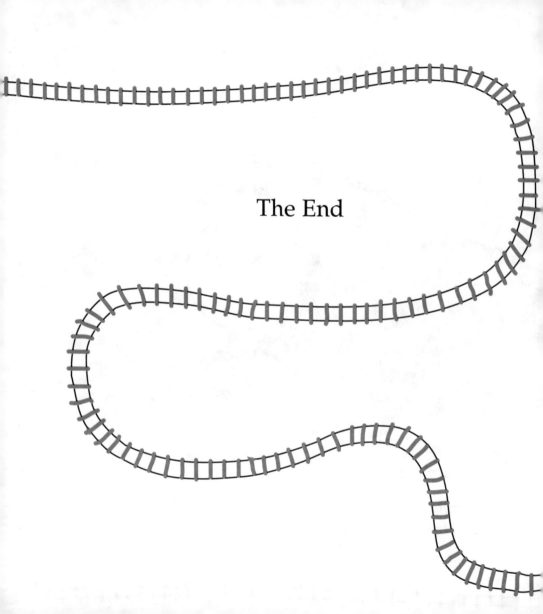

The End

Jellybean Books™ to Read and Love:

ISBN 0-679-89237-0

9 780679 892373

50199>

EAN